To

....

with love from

....

Written by Katherine Sully
Illustrated by Janet Samuel

First published 2007 by Parragon Books, Ltd.
Copyright © 2018 Cottage Door Press, LLC
5005 Newport Drive, Rolling Meadows, Illinois 60008
All Rights Reserved

10 9 8 7 6 5 4 3 2 1

ISBN 978-1-68052-550-2

Parragon Books is an imprint of Cottage Door Press, LLC.
Parragon Books® and the Parragon® logo are
registered trademarks of Cottage Door Press, LLC.

Where, Oh Where Is Huggle Buggle Bear?

Parragon.

Where, oh where is **Huggle Buggle** Bear?
I can't find him anywhere!
He always hides when it's time for bed.
He is such a **funny** bear!

Is he snacking on toast and honey,
Making crumbs with **Babbity Bunny**?

No!
He isn't with
Babbity Bunny.

Huggle Buggle knows it's bedtime
But this happens every night!
I can't go to bed without him.
It just would not be right.

Where, oh where is **Huggle Buggle** Bear?
I can't find him anywhere!
He always hides when it's time for bed.
He is such a **silly** bear!

Is he bouncing on his belly,
On the sofa with Ellie Nellie?

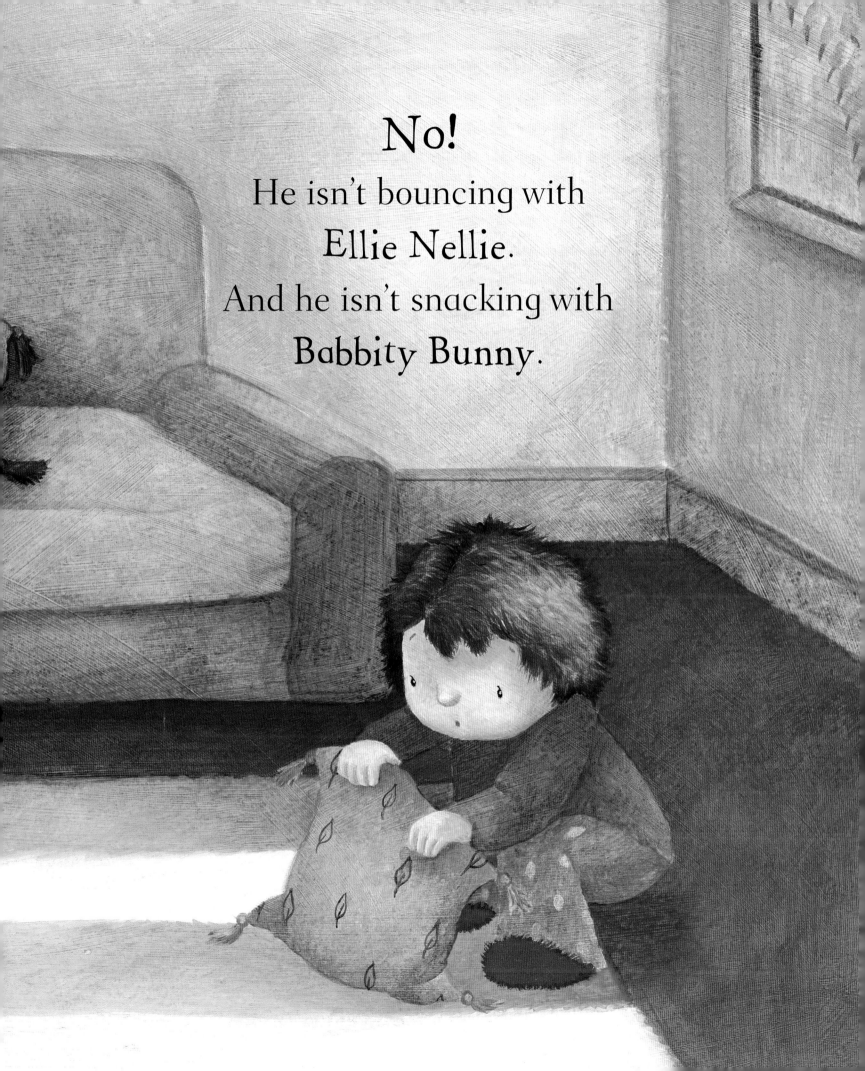

No!
He isn't bouncing with
Ellie Nellie.
And he isn't snacking with
Babbity Bunny.

It's way past **Huggle Buggle**'s bedtime
And I'm starting to feel sleepy.
I can't go to bed without him,
It's much too dark and creepy.

Where, oh where is Huggle Buggle Bear?
I can't find him anywhere!
He always hides when it's time for bed.
He is such a **naughty** bear!

Is he making lots of noise
With Woolly Lamb and the other toys?

No!

He isn't playing with
Woolly Lamb.
He isn't bouncing with
Ellie Nellie.
He isn't snacking with
Babbity Bunny.

It's way past **Huggle Buggle**'s bedtime
And I'm feeling worried now.
I can't go to bed without him.
I don't think that I know how.

Where, oh where is **Huggle Buggle** Bear?
I can't find him anywhere!
He always hides when it's time for bed.
He is such a **troublesome** bear.

Is he splashing in the tub,
Blowing bubbles with Rubadub?

No!
He isn't splashing with
Rubadub.
He isn't playing with
Woolly Lamb.
He isn't bouncing with
Ellie Nellie.
He isn't snacking with
Babbity Bunny.

It's way past **Huggle Buggle**'s bedtime
And now I'm feeling sad.
I don't want to go to bed without him,
It would make me feel so bad!

I know where...
there's Huggle Buggle Bear!
And here are all the other toys.
I think they must be fast asleep,
So, **sssh!** Don't make any noise!

Night-night!